Rusty

Based on *The Railway Series* by the Rev. W. Awdry

Illustrations by
Robin Davies and Jerry Smith

EGMONT

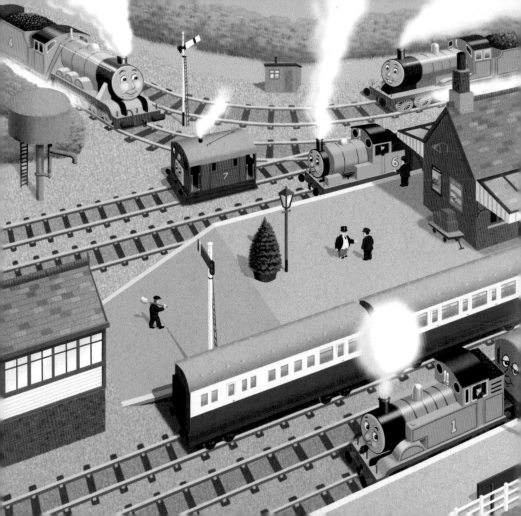

EGMONT

We bring stories to life

First published in Great Britain 2006
by Egmont UK Limited
239 Kensington High Street, London W8 6SA

Thomas the Tank Engine & Friends™

A BRITT ALLCROFT COMPANY PRODUCTION

Based on The Railway Series by The Reverend W Awdry
© 2006 Gullane (Thomas) LLC. A HIT Entertainment Company

Thomas the Tank Engine & Friends and Thomas & Friends are trademarks of Gullane (Thomas) Limited.
Thomas the Tank Engine & Friends and Design is Reg. US. Pat. & Tm. Off.

ISBN 978 1 4052 2656 1
ISBN 1 4052 2656 0
1 3 5 7 9 10 8 6 4 2
Printed in Great Britain

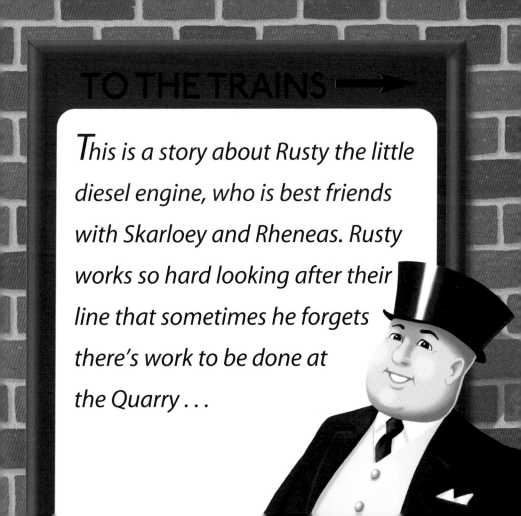

TO THE TRAINS →

This is a story about Rusty the little diesel engine, who is best friends with Skarloey and Rheneas. Rusty works so hard looking after their line that sometimes he forgets there's work to be done at the Quarry . . .

One autumn evening, Rusty returned late to the Quarry. The Fat Controller was cross.

"I'm sorry, Sir," said Rusty. "I was helping Rheneas and Skarloey on their mountain line."

"Their line is in bad condition," The Fat Controller explained. "Mending it takes up too much of your time. I am going to shut down the line."

Rusty was very upset.

"Rheneas and Skarloey will come and work here at the Quarry with you," said The Fat Controller. He had made up his mind.

The line was closed down the very next day and Rheneas and Skarloey arrived at the Quarry to work there instead.

They worked as hard as they could but they missed the forests and hills along their mountain line. Most of all, though, they missed their passengers.

Rusty could see they were not happy.

The next day, The Fat Controller came to the Quarry with some important news.

"We are going to be blasting here for the next two weeks," he said. "It won't be safe for you. I will find work for you to do somewhere else."

"Please, Sir," said Rusty. "May we go back to the old line and try to repair it? Then Rheneas and Skarloey can do their old jobs again."

The Fat Controller agreed. "But you must be back at the Quarry in two weeks' time," he warned the engines.

Rheneas and Skarloey's line was in a mess. It was covered with rocks and branches and the tracks were broken in several places.

The three little engines set to work straight away.

"There's no time to lose," said Rusty.

When Elizabeth the Vintage Lorry puffed past, she thought Rusty's plan to clear the tracks was silly. "What a waste of time!" she sniffed.

Skarloey was sad. "She's right," he said. "We'll never get all the work done in two weeks."

"We can't give up!" said Rusty.

The days passed and still the line was not fixed. The engines worked harder than ever but time was running out.

"It's no good," cried Rheneas.

"There's too much to do," moaned Skarloey.

But Rusty would not give up. He had a very clever idea.

The next day, Rusty saw Elizabeth trundling by. "If only we had a lorry to help us," he said loudly.

Elizabeth stopped. "I couldn't possibly help you," she said. "I'm a Quarry lorry."

"Well, we need a very special lorry," Rusty teased. "One that can haul and pull heavy branches."

"I *am* a very special lorry," snorted Elizabeth. "I can haul and pull!" she said proudly.

"So you'll do it?" said Rusty.

"I will!" smiled Elizabeth.

Elizabeth was as good as her word.

She hauled rubbish and pulled branches from the line.

She helped remove a fallen tree from the cattle crossing.

The little lorry puffed up and down helping the engines until all the work was done.

Together, they had finished the repairs with a day to spare!

"Thank you, Elizabeth," said Rusty.

"We couldn't have done it without you," said Rheneas and Skarloey together. "You are a very special lorry."

"I know!" puffed Elizabeth, importantly.

Rusty's crew finished sweeping up until everything was spick and span. The line had never looked so splendid!

Then Rusty's Driver telephoned The Fat Controller, who promised to inspect the line the next morning.

When The Fat Controller arrived, he was very pleased. "Well done, Rusty," he said. "And well done, Elizabeth. We will reopen the line straight away."

Rusty was very proud. Rheneas and Skarloey were very happy, too. They were looking forward to seeing their passengers again!

"Now you will have time to work at the Quarry for a change!" The Fat Controller told Rusty.

Rheneas and Skarloey went back to work on their old line, and Rusty went to the Quarry.

Rusty and Elizabeth have become firm friends.

Each time Elizabeth visits the Quarry, she greets Rusty with a friendly "Toot! Toot!" on her horn. She thinks Rusty is very special, too.

The Thomas Story Library is THE definitive collection of stories about Thomas and ALL his Friends.

5 more Thomas Story Library titles will be chuffing into your local bookshop in April 2007:

Arthur
Caroline
Murdoch
Neville
Freddie

And there are even more
Thomas Story Library books to follow later!
So go on, start your Thomas Story Library NOW!

A Fantastic Offer for Thomas the Tank Engine Fans!

In every Thomas Story Library book like this one, you will find a special token. Collect 6 Thomas tokens and we will send you a brilliant Thomas poster, and a double-sided bedroom door hanger!
Simply tape a £1 coin in the space above, and fill out the form overleaf.

TO BE COMPLETED BY AN ADULT

To apply for this great offer, ask an adult to complete the coupon below
and send it with a pound coin and 6 tokens, to:
THOMAS OFFERS, PO BOX 715, HORSHAM RH12 5WG

☐ Please send a Thomas poster and door hanger. I enclose 6 tokens
    plus a £1 coin. (Price includes P&P)

Fan's name...

Address..

....Postcode..............................

Date of birth..

Name of parent/guardian..

Signature of parent/guardian...

Please allow 28 days for delivery. Offer is only available while stocks last. We reserve the right to change
the terms of this offer at any time and we offer a 14 day money back guarantee. This does not affect your
statutory rights.

☐ Data Protection Act: If you do not wish to receive other similar offers from us or companies we
    recommend, please tick this box. Offers apply to UK only.